Lewis Carroll's Alice in Wonderland

Retold by Jane Carruth

 GOLDEN PRESS · NEW YORK
Western Publishing Company, Inc.
Racine, Wisconsin

Copyright © 1976 ibp Intercontinental Book Productions
U.S. edition published 1976 by Golden Press, New York. Western Publishing Company, Inc.
All rights reserved. Golden, A Golden Book ® and Golden Press ® are trademarks of Western Publishing Company, Inc.
Library of Congress Catalog Card Number 76 5920
ISBN 0 307 14755 X
Printed in Italy.

Down the Rabbit-hole

IT WAS SUCH a hot day — such a very hot day! Alice yawned. How boring it was to sit there on the bank beside her sister, who was reading a book which didn't even have any pictures in it.

Alice was just beginning to wonder if she should start making a daisy-chain to pass the time when, suddenly, a white rabbit with pink eyes ran close to her.

There was nothing so very remarkable in that; nor did Alice think so. But then she heard it say to itself, "Oh, dear, oh dear! I shall be too late!" and saw it take a watch out of its waistcoat-pocket and look at it before hurrying on. Well, that *was* remarkable. It was so remarkable that Alice scrambled to her feet and ran after it across the field, just in time to see the white rabbit pop down a large rabbit-hole under the hedge.

In another moment down went Alice after it. The rabbit-hole went straight on like a tunnel and then dipped suddenly down. "It's like — like falling downwards into a deep well," Alice said aloud. "But much slower and nicer," she added, as her eyes rested on the maps and pictures that decorated the sides of the hole. "I'm falling so slowly that I have time to see everything!"

Down, down, down. Would the fall *never* come to an end? Alice began to wonder if she was going to fall right through the earth. That would be funny for then she would come out among people walking on their heads!

"Dinah will miss me very much to-night," she said aloud. "She's such a friendly little cat. I hope they'll remember her saucer of milk at tea-time . . ." She began thinking so hard about Dinah that the sudden thump, thump of her landing came as quite a surprise.

"Well, I've arrived somewhere at last," said Alice, jumping up on her feet and finding that she was not in the least hurt. Overhead was all dark, but stretching before her was another long passage, and there was the white rabbit hurrying down it.

Away went Alice like the wind, and was just in time to hear it say, as it turned a

corner, "Oh, my ears and whiskers, how late it's getting!"

She was close behind it when she turned the corner, but the rabbit was no longer to be seen. Looking about her, she saw that she was in a long, low hall, lit by a row of lamps hanging from the roof.

There were doors all round the hall, but they were all locked, and Alice began to wonder sadly how she was ever going to escape. Then, she came upon a little three-legged table, made of solid glass, with

nothing on it except a tiny golden key. To her delight, the little golden key fitted exactly into the lock of a tiny door no more than fifteen inches high.

Alice opened the door and found that it led into a small passage, not much larger than a rat-hole. She knelt down and looked along the passage into the loveliest garden you ever saw. How she longed to get out of that dark hall, and wander about among those beds of bright flowers and sit by those cool fountains, but she could not even get her head through the doorway!

"I wish I could shut up like a telescope," thought poor Alice. And she got to her feet and went back to the table, half-hoping she might find another key on it. Instead, she found a little bottle ("which certainly was not here before," said Alice), and round its neck a paper label, with the words "DRINK ME" beautifully printed on it in large letters.

That was all very well, but Alice was too

wise to drink it without first making certain that the bottle was not marked "Poison", or the contents would almost certainly disagree with her, sooner or later.

However, this bottle was *not* marked "Poison", so Alice ventured to taste it, and finding it very nice, having a sort of mixed flavor of cherry-tart, custard, roast turkey, toffee and hot buttered toast, she very soon finished it off.

"What a curious feeling!" said Alice. "I must be shutting up like a telescope."

And so she was, for now she was only ten inches high. "Now, I'm the right size to go through the little door into that lovely garden," she reflected, "if only I could reach up to that little golden key."

She could see it quite plainly through the glass, and she tried her best to climb up one of the table-legs, but it was too slippery; and when she had tired herself out with trying, she sat down and began to cry.

Through her tears, she suddenly noticed a little glass box that was lying under the table. She opened it, and found in it a very small cake, on which the words "EAT ME" were beautifully marked in currants. "Well, I will eat you," said Alice, "and if it makes me larger, I can reach the key, and if it makes me smaller, I can creep under the door."

She ate a little bit; nothing happened, and with a disappointed sigh, she set to work and very soon finished off the cake.

The Caucus-race

Now, SUDDENLY, I'm opening out like the largest telescope that ever was!" cried Alice, as she began to shoot upwards. "Goodbye, feet!"

In another moment her head struck against the roof of the hall, and being now more than nine feet high, she was able to bend down and pick up the little golden key.

Poor Alice! It was as much as she could do, lying down on one side, to look through into that pretty garden with one eye. To reach it was more hopeless than ever. And feeling quite miserable, she sat up and began to cry again. On and on she cried, shedding gallons of tears, until there was a large pool all round her, about four inches deep, and reaching halfway down the hall.

After a time, she heard a pattering of feet in the distance, and she dried her eyes to see what was coming. It was the White Rabbit returning, splendidly dressed, with a pair of white kid gloves in one hand and a large fan in the other. As he came trotting along in a great hurry, he muttered to himself, "The Duchess, the Duchess! Oh, won't she be savage if I've kept her waiting!"

When the Rabbit came near her, Alice began, in a timid voice, "If you please, sir . . ." The Rabbit started violently, dropped the white kid gloves and the fan, and scurried away into the darkness as fast as he could go.

Alice picked up the gloves and fan, and to her surprise found that she was beginning to shrink. "It must be the fan," she told herself. "How very curious! But if I continue to hold it I'll probably shrink away to nothing." And she dropped it hastily — only just in time — for by now she was little more than two feet high.

Thankful for her narrow escape, she ran with all speed back to the little door, but

the door was shut, and the golden key was lying on the glass table as before and quite out of reach.

"Goodness," thought Alice, "matters are certainly going from bad to worse."

As she said these words her foot slipped, and in another moment, splash! She was up to her chin in salt water. "I wish I hadn't cried so much," Alice told herself, as she swam about, trying to find her way out of the pool. "It would be awful if I drowned in my own tears!"

Just then she heard something splashing about a little way off, and she swam nearer to make out what it was; at first she thought it must be a walrus or a hippopotamus, but then she remembered her own tiny size, and she soon made out that it was only a mouse that had slipped into the water like herself.

After trying to make conversation with the mouse in English, Alice decided it must be a French mouse. *"Ou est ma chatte?"* she began, remembering the first sentence in her French grammar book.

At this, the mouse gave a sudden leap out of the water, and seemed to quiver all over with fright.

"Oh, I beg your pardon," cried Alice quickly. "I quite forgot that you didn't like cats."

"Would you like cats if *you* were me?" cried the mouse, in a shrill, passionate voice. "Would you?"

"Well, perhaps not," said Alice in a soothing tone. "Though I think you would like Dinah ..." But the mouse was swimming away from her as hard as it could. It was by no means easy now to swim anywhere very far, for the pool was now quite crowded with the birds and animals that had fallen into it; there were a duck and a dodo, a lory and an eaglet, and several other curious creatures. Finally, Alice began making for the shore, and the whole party swam after her.

They made an odd-looking party as they gathered on the bank, for all were dripping wet, cross and uncomfortable.

"The first thing to do," said the Dodo, "is to get dry. We'll have a Caucus-race."

"What *is* a Caucus-race?" Alice asked, in the silence that followed.

"Why," said the Dodo, "the best way to explain it is to do it."

And he began marking out a race-course, in a sort of circle. Then all the party was placed along the course, here and there. There was no "One, two, three, go!" Everybody just began running when they liked, and left off when they liked, so that it was not easy to know when the race was over. However, when they had been running half an hour or so, and were quite dry again, the Dodo suddenly called out, "The race is over!"

"You must give the prizes," said the Dodo, pointing at Alice, and the whole party crowded round her.

In despair, Alice put her hand in her pocket and pulled out a box of comfits, which she handed round as prizes. It was lucky there was a sweet for everyone. Then, to satisfy the Dodo, she gave him her little silver thimble, which he solemnly presented back to her, so that she too could say she had received a prize.

"Oh, I wish I had Dinah here to join in the fun!" cried Alice. "She's the dearest cat imaginable, and a capital one at catching mice. And oh, I wish you could see her after the birds! Why, she'll eat a bird as soon as look at it."

Her words had a remarkable effect on the party. Many of the birds hurried off at once, while others of the company declared it was high time they were in bed, and moved away. Soon, poor Alice found herself alone again and, feeling miserable and upset, could not hold back her tears.

Presently, as she wept, she heard the patter of little feet, and looking up, saw the White Rabbit trotting towards her.

Inside the White Rabbit's House

AT FIRST THE White Rabbit paid no attention to Alice. His face wore an anxious expression as he began looking around.

Then Alice heard him mutter, "Where can I have dropped them?" And she guessed that he was searching for the gloves and fan, so she got up and began hunting around too, noticing as she did so that the great hall, the glass table and the little door had vanished completely.

Presently the Rabbit noticed Alice and called out to her in an angry voice, "Why, Mary Ann, what *are* you doing out here? Run home this moment and fetch me another pair of gloves and a fan! Quick, now!" And Alice was so much frightened by his tone that she ran off at once in the direction the Rabbit pointed.

"How surprised he'll be when he finds out that I am *not* his housemaid after all," she said to herself, as she came upon a neat little house, on the door of which was a bright brass plate with the name

"W. Rabbit" engraved upon it. Then in she went without knocking and ran upstairs.

The room at the top of the stairs was small and tidy, and on the table in the window lay a fan and two or three pairs of tiny white kid gloves. Just as she took up the fan and a pair of the gloves, her eyes fell on a little bottle that stood near the looking-glass. "Whenever I eat or drink anything," she said to herself, "something interesting happens. I do hope it will make me grow larger again for I'm quite tired of being such a tiny little thing." And she uncorked the bottle and put it to her lips.

Something *did* happen. Before she had drunk half the bottle, she found her head pressing against the ceiling, and she had to stoop to prevent her neck from being broken. She put down the bottle quickly, wishing she had not drunk quite so much.

There was now no chance of her ever getting out of the room again, and she began to feel more unhappy than ever. Presently, as she lay on her side, she heard a voice outside.

"Mary Ann! Mary Ann!" said the voice. "Fetch me my gloves this moment." Then came the pattering of feet on the stairs, and Alice knew it was the Rabbit come to look for her. She trembled so much that she shook the house, quite forgetting that she was now a thousand times as big as the Rabbit, and had no reason to be afraid of him.

When the Rabbit reached the door, he tried to open it, but Alice's elbow was pressed hard against it, and so he was quite unable to do so.

"I'll go round and get in by the window," Alice heard the Rabbit say angrily.

"That you won't do," thought Alice, and, after waiting till she fancied she heard the Rabbit under the window, she suddenly spread out her hand, and made a snatch in the air outside the window.

There was a little shriek and the crash of breaking glass — and then silence.

After some time, Alice heard voices again. "Here, Bill! Catch hold of this rope . . . Will the roof hold? Mind that loose slate. Now, Bill, you're the one the master says is to go down the chimney . . ."

"Oh! So Bill, whoever he is, means to come down the chimney," Alice said to herself. "Well, this fireplace is narrow, to be sure, but I think I can kick a little!"

She waited until she heard the little animal scratching and scrambling about in the chimney close above her foot, then she gave one sharp kick and waited to see what would happen next.

The first thing she heard was a chorus of "There goes Bill!" — then another voice crying, "Catch him by the hedge!"

After another silence, the Rabbit's voice came sharp and clear: "We must burn the house down!" And Alice called out as loud as she could, "If you do, I'll set Dinah at you!"

After what seemed to Alice a very long time, a shower of little pebbles came rattling in at the window, some of them hitting her in the face, and she shouted again, "You'd better stop doing that!" which produced another dead silence.

Then she noticed with some surprise that the pebbles were all turning into little cakes as they lay on the floor, and a bright idea came into her head. "If I eat one of these cakes, it's more than likely I'll get smaller!" she thought. And she swallowed one of the cakes. To her delight she found that she was beginning to shrink quite rapidly.

As soon as she was small enough to get through the door, she ran out of the house. At the sight of her, the crowd of animals and birds waiting outside set up a great cry and began chasing after her — all except for poor little Lizard Bill, who had turned a very pale green and was being held up by two guinea-pigs!

Alice set off running as hard as she could until she found herself in a thick wood, where she felt reasonably safe. "The first thing I've got to do," said Alice to herself, as she began walking through the long grass, "is to grow to my proper size again. I suppose I ought to eat or drink something or other; but the great question is, what?"

Advice from a Caterpillar

As ALICE LOOKED around her at the flowers and tall blades of grass, she suddenly saw a large mushroom, about the same height as herself. And stretching herself up on tiptoe, she found herself staring at a huge blue caterpillar, who was sitting on the top, arms folded, quietly smoking a hookah.

The Caterpillar took the hookah out of his mouth, and said in a low, sleepy voice, "Who are *you?*"

This was not a very encouraging opening for a conversation, and Alice replied, rather shyly, "I — I hardly know, sir. I know who I *was* when I got up this morning, but I think I must have changed several times since then. I *do* wish I could stay the same size."

But the Caterpillar merely repeated his question, and Alice began to feel a little annoyed. "Perhaps," she said, "you would tell me who *you* are?"

"Why?" said the Caterpillar. "I don't see why I should!"

"Well, I should like to be a *little* larger, sir, if you wouldn't mind," said Alice. "Three inches is such a wretched height to be."

"It is a very good height indeed!" said the Caterpillar angrily, rearing himself upright as he spoke. "That's my height exactly! You'll get used to it."

"But I'm *not* used to it," pleaded poor Alice. And she waited patiently while the Caterpillar yawned once or twice, and shook himself. Then he got down from the mushroom, and crawled away into the grass, merely remarking as he went, "One side will make you grow taller, and the other side will make you grow shorter."

"He must mean the mushroom," Alice told herself, and she looked at it thoughtfully, trying to decide which were the two sides of it. Finally, she stretched her arms round it as far as they would go, and broke off a bit of the edge with each hand.

"Now we'll see," said she, nibbling from the bit of mushroom in her right hand. The next moment she felt a violent blow underneath her chin — it had struck her foot!

A good deal frightened, she began to eat some of the mushroom in her left hand, and to her relief and delight found herself growing. But then she went on growing — at quite an alarming rate until, presently, her shoulders disappeared among the leaves of some tall trees, and her neck was

The creature seemed so determined to be unhelpful that, disappointed, Alice turned away. But then he called her back. "Keep your temper," said the Caterpillar. "What size do you want to be?" And he began puffing away at his hookah, while Alice searched for an answer.

At length she said, "I'm not really particular. I'd just like to stop changing so often."

"Are you content now?" asked the Caterpillar, taking the hookah out of his mouth.

so long that she found she could weave it in and out among the branches in the manner of a serpent.

As well as she could, she crouched down among the trees, and after a while she remembered that she still held the pieces of mushroom in her hands, and she set to work very carefully, nibbling first at one and then at the other, until she had succeeded in bringing herself down to her usual height.

It was so long since she had been anything like her proper size, that Alice felt quite strange at first. But she soon got used to it and, after a moment, began talking to herself, as usual. "The next thing," she said, "is to try and find a way to get into that beautiful garden. I wonder how I am going to manage it?"

Just as she said this, she came upon a little open space in the wood with a little house in it that was just about as tall as herself.

"I wonder who lives there?" she asked herself. "Whoever it is must be a good deal smaller than me, so I'd better do something about it."

And she took a piece of mushroom from the right-hand pocket of her dress and began to nibble at it until she was no more than some nine inches tall.

Alice Meets the Duchess

As she stood looking at the house for a minute or two, a footman — at least, Alice thought that was what he must be, though he looked more like a fish — came running out of the wood.

He knocked loudly on the door, which was opened by another footman, with a round face, and large eyes like a frog.

Alice noticed that both the Fish-Footman and the Frog-Footman wore very grand uniforms, and that they both had powdered hair that curled all over their heads.

The Fish-Footman then brought out from under his arm a letter which was almost as big as himself, and handed it over to the Frog-Footman, saying in a loud and solemn voice, "For the Duchess. An invitation from the Queen to play croquet."

Then they both bowed low — so low that their heads touched and their curls got entangled together.

Alice laughed so much at this that she had to run back into the woods in case they heard her, and when at last she came out of her hiding-place behind a tree, she found that the Fish-Footman had gone, and the Frog-Footman was sitting on the ground near the door, staring up into the sky.

"There's no sense in knocking," said the Footman as Alice went up to the door and lifted the knocker.

"Why not?" said Alice.

"For two reasons," said the Footman. "First, because I'm on the same side of the door as you are, and so cannot answer your knock. And second, because they're making such a noise inside, no one could possibly hear you — certainly not the Duchess!"

"There certainly does seem to be something going on inside," Alice said. "There's a good deal of crashing and banging — and sneezing. But tell me, how am I to get in?"

But the Frog-Footman wasn't listening. "You might knock if you were *inside*," he said dreamily, "and then I could let you out. Or if I were inside you could let *me* out . . ."

"But you *are* out — we're *both* outside," Alice interrupted impatiently. "Just tell me how I am to get inside!"

"For my part," said the Footman, staring up into the sky, "I shall sit here until tomorrow . . ."

At this moment the door of the little house suddenly opened, and a large plate came skimming out, straight at the Footman's head.

Deciding that she would get no help from the Footman, who was now nursing a grazed nose, Alice opened the door herself and went in.

The door led straight into a large kitchen, which was full of smoke. On a three-legged stool sat the Duchess nursing a baby. The cook was leaning over the fire, stirring a large cauldron which seemed to be full of soup.

"There's certainly too much pepper in that soup," Alice said to herself, as she began to sneeze.

There was certainly too much pepper in the air, too, for even the Duchess was sneezing now, and the baby. The only ones in the kitchen who were not sneezing were the cook, and a large cat which was sitting on the hearth grinning from ear to ear.

"Please, would you tell me," began Alice, a little timidly, "why your cat grins like that?"

"It's a Cheshire cat," said the Duchess, "and that's why. Pig!"

Alice quite jumped at this — then she saw that the Duchess was looking down at the baby, and not at her.

Without warning, the cook suddenly took the cauldron of soup off the fire, and began throwing everything within her reach at the Duchess and the baby. The fire-irons came first; then a shower of saucepans, plates and dishes. The Duchess took no notice of them even when they hit her; she kept tossing the baby violently up and down until, at last, she flung it at Alice, saying, "I must go and get ready to play croquet with the Queen."

Alice only just caught the baby, which was snorting like a steam-engine and kicking out in all directions. She carried it outside at once to get some fresh air.

When it quieted down, it began to grunt, and Alice saw that it had a *very* turned-up nose, and extremely small eyes for a baby. Just when she was beginning to think that it must be a pig after all, it jumped down from her lap and quietly trotted away into the woods.

Greatly relieved to be rid of her charge so easily, Alice got to her feet and was wondering where to go next, when she saw the Cheshire Cat sitting on the bough of a tree a few yards off.

The Cat only grinned when it saw Alice. "Cheshire Puss," said she, "What sort of people live about here, please?"

"In *that* direction," the Cat said, waving its right paw round, "lives the Hatter; and in *that* direction," waving the other paw, "lives a March Hare. Visit whichever you like — they're both mad."

"But — but I don't want to go among mad people," Alice remarked.

"Oh, you can't help that," said the Cat. "We're all mad here. By the way, are you playing croquet with the Queen today?"

"I should like that very much," said Alice, "but I haven't been invited."

"*I'll* be there," said the Cat, vanishing.

While she was still looking at the place where it had been, it suddenly appeared again. "By the bye, what became of the baby?" said the Cat. "I forgot to ask."

"It turned into a pig," Alice answered.

"I thought so," it said, vanishing again.

A second later, it was back. "Did you say 'pig' or 'fig'?"

"I said 'pig'," replied Alice. "You make me giddy, vanishing so suddenly."

"Sorry," said the Cat. This time it vanished quite slowly, beginning with the tail-end and ending ·with the grin, which remained some time after the rest had gone.

"That's the most curious thing I ever saw in my life," she said, going through the woods to find the March Hare.

A Mad Tea-party

ALICE WAS in no doubt that she had found the March Hare's house when she suddenly came upon it, for the chimneys were shaped like ears and the roof was thatched with fur. It was such a big house that she hastily nibbled some of the left-hand bit of mushroom which she still had, to increase her height.

Under a tree, she saw a table set out with tea things. Sitting at it were the March Hare and the Hatter. Between them was a fat Dormouse, fast asleep. Although the table was very long, all three were crowded together at one corner of it, and when the March Hare and the Hatter noticed Alice approaching, they both cried, "No room! No room!"

"There's plenty of room," said Alice indignantly, and she sat down in a large armchair at one end of the table.

"Have some wine," the March Hare suddenly said.

"I don't see any wine," Alice said, "only tea."

"That's because there isn't any," said the March Hare.

"Then you shouldn't offer it," said Alice angrily.

"Your hair wants cutting," said the Hatter, joining in the conversation.

"It's very rude to make personal remarks," said Alice severely.

The Hatter opened his eyes very wide at this, but all he said was, "Why is a raven like a writing-desk?"

Alice began to smile; there was nothing she liked better than riddles.

The party sat silent for a minute, while Alice thought over all she could remember about ravens and writing-desks, which wasn't much.

The Hatter was the first to break the silence. "What day of the month is it?" he asked, turning to Alice. And he took his watch out of his pocket and shook it, before holding it to his ear.

"The fourth," said Alice.

"Wrong," sighed the Hatter. "I told you butter wouldn't suit the works!" he added looking crossly at the March Hare.

"It was the *best* butter," the March Hare meekly replied. "The very best!"

"Yes, but some crumbs must have got in as well," the Hatter grumbled. "You shouldn't have put it in with the bread knife."

The March Hare took the watch and looked at it gloomily. Then he dipped it into his cup of tea and looked at it again, but could think of nothing better to say than, "It *was* the best butter."

"The Dormouse is asleep again," said the Hatter suddenly, and he poured a little hot tea on its nose. "Have you guessed the riddle yet?" he went on, turning to Alice.

Alice shook her head, and he sighed. "Never mind — it's always tea-time here, you know!"

"Is that why so many tea things are laid out?" asked Alice. "You just keep on moving round the table."

"Exactly so," said the Hatter. "It's been like this ever since he —" and he pointed to the March Hare — "went mad. Quite mad, you know."

"I think I see," said Alice brightly. "You never wash up, I suppose?"

"Of course not," said the Hatter. "Let's all move one place on. I want a clean cup."

He moved on as he spoke, and the Dormouse opened its eyes and followed him. The March Hare moved into the Dormouse's place, and Alice rather unwillingly took the March Hare's.

The Hatter then pinched the Dormouse to stop it falling asleep again and told it to tell them a story.

No one paid Alice the slightest attention and when she did try to talk, the Hatter snapped, "Don't talk, keep quiet!"

At this rudeness, Alice got up in great disgust and walked off. The last thing she saw them trying to do was to put the Dormouse into the teapot.

"At any rate I'll never go there again!" said Alice, as she made her way through the wood. "It's the stupidest tea-party I ever was at in all my life."

Just as she said this, she noticed that one of the trees had a door leading right into it. "That's very curious!" she thought. "I may as well go in at once." And in she went.

Once more she found herself in the long hall, standing close to the little glass table. She took the little golden key and unlocked the door that led into the beautiful garden. Then she set to work nibbling at the mushroom in her right-hand pocket until she was small enough to go through the door and walk down the little passage.

Now, at last, she was in the beautiful garden, among the bright flower-beds and the cool fountains!

The King and Queen of Hearts

As soon as Alice entered the garden the first thing she noticed was a large rose-tree. The roses on it were white, but three gardeners were busily painting them red.

"That's very curious," Alice thought, as she stood watching them. "Very curious indeed!"

Then she heard one of the painters say, "Look out now, Five! Don't go splashing paint over me like that."

"I couldn't help it," Five answered sulkily. "Seven jogged my elbow. Honestly, Two!"

"That's right, blame me!" said Seven, putting down his brush. "Always blame others . . ."

"You'd better not talk!" said Five. "I heard the Queen say only yesterday you deserved to be beheaded!"

"What the Queen says and does not say," said Two, "is none of our business . . ." He stopped suddenly when he noticed Alice watching. Then he bowed to her in a most courteous way, and so did the others.

"Would you tell me, please," said Alice, greatly flattered, "why you are painting those roses?"

"Why, the fact is, Miss," said Two, "this here tree should have had red roses; we put a white rose-tree here by mistake. If the Queen was to find out, we should all have our heads cut off. So you see, Miss, we're doing our best before she comes . . ."

At this moment Five, who had been anxiously looking across the garden, called out, "The Queen! The Queen!" And the three gardeners instantly threw themselves flat upon their faces.

There was a sound of many footsteps, and Alice, feeling very sorry for the three frightened gardeners, looked round, anxious to see the terrible Queen.

First came ten soldiers carrying clubs; these were all shaped like the three gardeners, oblong and flat, with their hands and feet at the corners. Next came ten courtiers, ornamented all over with diamonds, and walking in pairs as the soldiers did. They were followed by the royal children, jumping merrily along and holding hands, and they, too, were ornamented all over with hearts.

Alice waited eagerly for the Queen, but next in the royal procession came the

guests, mostly kings and queens, and among them the White Rabbit. Then came the Knave of Hearts carrying the King's crown on a crimson velvet cushion; and then, the very last in the procession, came the King and Queen of Hearts.

Alice began to wonder if she should lie down on her face like the gardeners. Then she thought that it really wouldn't do if everybody lay down whenever a procession was coming, for then it wouldn't be seen at all.

"I'll just stay where I am," she said to herself, "and wait and see what happens."

As soon as the Queen reached Alice, she stopped and looked at her severely, and the whole procession stood still.

"Who is this?" demanded the Queen, turning to the Knave of Hearts, who bowed and smiled but made no answer.

"My name is Alice, so please your Majesty," said Alice very politely. But she added, to herself, "Why, they're only a pack of cards, after all. I needn't be afraid of them."

"And who are *these?*" asked the Queen, pointing to the three gardeners who were lying round the rose-tree beside their pots of paint. As they were lying on their faces, the pattern on their backs was the same as the rest of the pack so it was quite impossible to make out who they were. They could have been three of the soldiers, or courtiers, or even three of their own children.

"How should I know?" said Alice,

But as three of the soldiers advanced on the gardeners, they ran to Alice for protection.

"I won't let them cut off your heads," she whispered. And she hurriedly put them into a large flower-pot that stood behind her. She did this so swiftly that the soldiers couldn't make out where the gardeners had vanished to. And, at length, they went to the Queen, who had walked away, and told her the executions had been performed.

The Queen looked back over her shoulder. "Can you play croquet?" she roared at Alice.

"Yes," Alice shouted back.

"Come on, then!" screamed the Queen,

surprising herself at her own boldness. "It's really no business of mine!"

The Queen turned red with rage at this, and after glaring at her for a moment, began screaming, "Off with her head! Off with her head . . ."

"Nonsense," said Alice very loudly. And the Queen stopped screaming.

Then the King laid a hand on her arm, and said in a timid voice, "She's only a child, my dear. Don't be too hard on her."

The Queen now turned her attention to the three gardeners. "Turn them over," she ordered the Knave, who did so, very carefully, with one foot.

"Get up!" shouted the Queen, in a harsh, shrill voice. And the gardeners jumped up and began bowing to the King and Queen, the royal children and everybody else in sight.

"Stop it!" the Queen ordered. "Stop this bowing and tell me what you were doing here."

"May it please your Majesty," said Two, in a very humble voice, "we were trying . . ."

"I see!" said the Queen, examining the roses. "Off with their heads!"

and Alice joined the procession, wondering what would happen next.

As she followed the Queen, she found she was walking beside the White Rabbit, who was peeping anxiously into her face.

"Where's the Duchess?" asked Alice.

"Hush, hush!" whispered the Rabbit, looking more anxious than ever. "She's under sentence of execution. You see, she — she boxed the Queen's ears . . ."

Alice gave a little giggle, and the Rabbit begged her, in a frightened whisper, to keep quiet and not attract the Queen's attention.

Presently, the procession came to a halt. The Queen shouted, "Get to your places," and people began running about in all directions. However, after a while, they all settled down and the game commenced.

Alice found herself playing the strangest kind of croquet imaginable. For one thing, the ground was all ridges and furrows, and for another, the croquet balls were live hedgehogs, and the mallets live flamingoes. All the soldiers were now bent double standing on their hands and feet to make arches.

The flamingo Alice found herself grasping kept looking up into her face with such a puzzled expression that she could not help but laugh. And besides, whenever she succeeded in getting its neck nicely straightened out so that she could give the hedgehog a blow, the hedgehog would unroll itself and crawl away.

All the players were quarrelling among themselves and fighting for the poor hedgehogs, and in a short time the Queen was in a furious passion, stamping about, and screaming, "Off with his head!" or "Off with her head!"

Alice was beginning to wish she could find some means of escape when, after about half an hour, all the players, except the King, the Queen and herself, were under sentence of execution.

She had set free her flamingo, and as she watched it flying in a helpless kind of way across the garden, the Queen came up to her, and gasped, "Have you seen the Mock Turtle yet?"

"No," said Alice. "I don't even know what a Mock Turtle is."

"It's what Mock Turtle Soup is made from," said the Queen. "I'll take you to the Gryphon, and he will take you to the Mock Turtle."

"I'd like that," said Alice. And she followed the Queen off the croquet ground, thankful to escape from such a silly game.

The Mock Turtle's Story

MUCH SOONER than Alice had expected, they came upon the Gryphon, lying fast asleep in the sun.

"Up, lazy thing!" said the Queen, "and take this young lady to see the Mock Turtle. I must go back and see about some executions I ordered." And she walked off, leaving Alice alone with the Gryphon.

Alice was not sure that she liked the look of the Gryphon, but on the whole it would be safer to stay with him than go after the savage Queen, so she stood quietly waiting for the creature to say something.

The Gryphon sat up and rubbed his eyes. Then he chuckled, half to himself and half to Alice. "She's funny, that one," he said. "They never execute nobody, you know, no matter what *she* says. Come on!"

They found the Mock Turtle, sitting sad and lonely on a little ledge of rock and, as they came nearer, Alice could hear him sighing as if his heart would break.

"What makes him so sad?" she asked the Gryphon.

The Gryphon said, "He hasn't got anything to make him sad. It's all in his mind. Come on, I'll introduce you."

So they went up to the Mock Turtle, who looked at them with large eyes full of tears.

"This here young lady," said the Gryphon, "wants for to know your history, she do."

"I'll tell it to her," said the Mock Turtle, in a deep hollow voice. "Sit down, both of you, and don't speak a word till I've finished."

So they sat down, and Alice waited patiently for the Mock Turtle to begin his story.

"Once," said he, after a long silence, "I was a real turtle."

There was another long silence, broken only by the Mock Turtle's sobbing, and Alice began to wonder if there was any more story to come.

After more heartbreaking sobs, the Mock Turtle went on, "When we were little we went to school in the sea. Our master was an old turtle — we used to call him Tortoise —"

"Why did you call him Tortoise, if he wasn't one?" Alice asked.

"We called him Tortoise because he *taught* us," replied the Mock Turtle angrily. "Really, you are very dull."

"You shouldn't have asked such a simple question," commented the Gryphon. "You ought to be ashamed of yourself." And poor Alice felt ready to sink into the earth.

"Go on with your story, old fellow," said the Gryphon, turning to the Mock Turtle. "Don't be all day about it."

"Yes, we went to school in the sea, though you may not believe it . . ." the Mock turtle began again, not looking at Alice. "We had the best education — in fact we went to school every day . . ."

"I've been to day-school, too," said Alice. "You needn't be so proud as all that."

"With extras?" asked the Mock Turtle, a little anxiously.

"Yes," said Alice, "we learned French and music."

"And washing?" asked the Mock Turtle.

"Certainly not!" said Alice indignantly.

"Ah, then yours wasn't a really good school," said the Mock Turtle, sounding greatly relieved.

"Get on with the story," said the Gryphon, and the Mock Turtle sighed deeply, and drew the back of one flapper across his eyes.

"You may not have lived much under the sea," he said, looking at Alice, who shook her head, "so you can have no idea what a delightful thing a Lobster Quadrille is!"

"No, indeed," said Alice. "What sort of a dance is it?"

"You form a line along the seashore," said the Mock Turtle, "with the lobsters as partners."

"You advance twice . . ." put in the Gryphon.

"Then you throw the . . ." the Mock Turtle went on, highly excited, "you throw the . . ."

"The lobsters!" shouted the Gryphon, with a bound into the air.

"As far out to sea as you can!" yelled

the Mock Turtle, leaping about like a mad thing.

"It must be a very pretty dance," said Alice at last, when the Mock Turtle was close enough to talk to.

"Would you like to see a little of it?" he asked as soon as he had got over his excitement a little. "You can do it without lobsters, you know. Watch!"

Then, the two creatures began solemnly to dance, round and round Alice, sometimes passing so close that they stood on her toes. They waved their forepaws to mark time to the sad little song which the Mock Turtle presently started to sing.

After the dance, Alice began telling them about her adventures, and the Mock Turtle sang another sad song called "Turtle Soup". Just when he was beginning on the second chorus, all three heard a shout of "The trial's beginning!"

"Come on!" cried the Gryphon and, taking Alice by the hand, he hurried off, without waiting for the end of the song.

"What trial is it?" Alice panted, as she ran at the Gryphon's side. "What trial?"

But the Gryphon only answered, "Come on!" and ran faster than ever.

Who Stole the Tarts?

ALICE HAD never been in a court of justice before, but she had read about them in books, and she was quite pleased to find that she knew the names of nearly everything there.

When they first arrived, they found themselves among a great crowd of little birds and beasts, as well as the whole pack of cards.

The King and Queen of Hearts were seated on their thrones. The Knave was standing before them in chains, with a soldier on each side to guard him; and near the King, Alice was delighted to see,

was the White Rabbit, with a trumpet in one hand and a scroll of parchment in the other.

In the middle of the court was a table, with a large dish of tarts upon it. The tarts made Alice feel quite hungry whenever she looked at them. "I wish they would get the trial done," she said to herself, "and then they could hand round the refreshments. I'd have one of these tarts!" But there seemed no chance of this, so she turned her attention to the judge in his great white curly wig.

The judge was the King himself, and as

he wore his crown over the great wig, he looked very uncomfortable and not a bit dignified.

There was nothing much the judge could do at this point, however, and Alice turned her attention to the twelve jurymen or jurors, feeling very pleased that she knew who they were, and why they were in court.

The jurors were made up of a strange assortment of birds and beasts, and they were all busily writing on slates.

"What are they doing?" Alice whispered to the Gryphon. "They can't have anything to put down yet, before the trial has begun."

"They're putting down their names,"

"The Queen of Hearts she made some tarts all on a Summer's day. The Knave of Hearts he stole those tarts and took them

the Gryphon whispered in reply, "in case they should forget them before the end of the trial."

"Stupid things!" Alice began in a loud, indignant voice, but she stopped herself hastily, for the White Rabbit suddenly cried out, "Silence in the court!" And the King put on his spectacles and looked anxiously round, to make out who was talking.

Alice then made her way round the court to the jurymen and saw that they were now scribbling on their slates the word "stupid".

"A fine muddle they will get into," she told herself, "when they come to read their slates after the trial. That word 'stupid' has nothing to do with the evidence."

One of the jurors had a pencil that squeaked and Alice, who could not stand squeaking pencils, bent over and snatched it away from him. The juror was poor little Bill the Lizard who could not make out where his pencil had got to. After hunting around for it, he was obliged to write with one finger for the rest of the trial — which was of very little use, as it left no mark on the slate.

Suddenly, the King stood up. "Herald," he shouted, "read the accusation!"

At this, the White Rabbit blew three blasts on the trumpet, then unrolled the parchment scroll and read as follows:
"The Queen of Hearts, she made some tarts,
All on a summer day:
The Knave of Hearts, he stole those tarts
And took them quite away!"

"Consider your verdict," said the King, addressing the jury.

"Not yet, not yet, sire," the Rabbit said quickly. "There is a great deal to come before that!"

"Call the first witness," said the King, as if he had not been interrupted. And the White Rabbit blew three blasts on the trumpet, and called out, "First witness! First witness!"

Alice went and sat down beside the Dormouse.

"I wish you wouldn't squeeze so," said the Dormouse. "I can hardly breathe."

"I can't help it," Alice said meekly.
"You see, I'm growing."

It was true, she was beginning to grow
again and getting larger all the time. But
as long as there was room for her in court,
she made up her mind to stay. Besides, she
must see who was to be the first witness.

It was the Hatter!

The Hatter came in with a tea-cup in
one hand and a piece of bread-and-butter
in the other.

"I beg your pardon, your Majesty," he
began, "for bringing these in, but I hadn't
quite finished my tea when I was sent for."

"You ought to have finished," said the
King. "When did you begin?"

The Hatter looked at the March Hare,
who had followed him into the court.

"Fourteenth of March, I think it was,"
he said.

"Fifteenth," said the March Hare.

"Sixteenth," piped up the Dormouse, from its seat.

"Write that down," said the King, addressing the jury, and the jurymen eagerly wrote down all three dates on their slates, then added them up.

"Take off your hat," the King said to the Hatter.

"It isn't mine," said the Hatter.

"Stolen!" the King exclaimed. "Make a note of that!"

"I keep them to sell," the Hatter added, by way of an explanation. "I've none of my own. I'm a hatter."

At this, the Queen put on her spectacles, and stared hard at the Hatter, who fidgeted and turned very pale.

He began shifting from one foot to the other, looking uneasily at the Queen. In his confusion, he bit a large piece out of his tea-cup instead of the bread-and-butter.

"Give your evidence," the King shouted angrily, "or I'll have you executed."

"I'm a poor man, your Majesty," the Hatter began in a trembling voice, "and I hadn't — but — just begun my tea — that is, not above a week or so, and what with bread-and-butter getting so thin, and . . . and . . ."

The miserable Hatter stopped altogether. He dropped his tea-cup and bread-and-butter, and went down on one knee.

"I'm a poor man, your Majesty," he repeated.

"You're a very poor speaker," said the King.

One of the two guinea-pigs present began to cheer at the King's words, and several officers of the court rushed over with a large canvas bag, which tied up at the mouth with strings. Into this they slipped the cheering guinea-pig, head first, and then sat on it.

"I'm glad I saw that done," Alice said to herself. "I've often wondered what they did when the public was too noisy in court."

Meanwhile the King was speaking again. "If that is all you know about the case of the stolen tarts," he said to the Hatter, who was still on one knee, "you may stand down."

"I can go no lower," said the Hatter. "I'm on the floor already."

"Then you may sit down," the King replied.

Here the other guinea-pig cheered, and was almost at once given the same treatment as his friend.

"That's the end of the guinea-pigs," Alice thought, as the Hatter ran from the court. "Now that the guinea-pigs are silenced, and the Hatter out of the way, let's hope the trial goes more quickly."

"Call the next witness!" said the King, and Alice looked round eagerly to see who it could be.

It was the Duchess's cook. She carried

the pepper-box in her hand, and as she advanced through the court all the people started to sneeze.

"Give your evidence," said the King, in the middle of a sneeze.

"Shan't," said the cook, defiantly.

The King looked anxiously at the White Rabbit, who said in a low voice, "Your Majesty must cross-examine this witness."

"Well, if I must, I must," the King said, and he folded his arms and frowned at the cook. Then he said in a deep voice, "What are the tarts made of?"

"Pepper, mostly," said the cook.

"Treacle," said a sleepy voice behind her.

"Collar that dormouse!" the Queen shrieked out. "Behead that dormouse. Turn that dormouse out of court. Off with his whiskers!"

For some minutes the whole court was

turning to the Queen, "must be the one to do the cross-examining."

Alice, who was growing very big by now, watched the White Rabbit as he fumbled over the list.

"I wonder who the next witness will be?" she asked herself. "They haven't heard anything of use, so far."

Imagine her surprise, when the White Rabbit read out, at the top of his shrill little voice, the name "Alice!"

in a turmoil, for the officers upset everyone as they tried to catch the Dormouse. By the time the Dormouse had been caught and taken away, the cook had disappeared.

"Never mind!" exclaimed the King, with a sigh of relief. "Call the next witness. And you, my dear," he added,

Alice Upsets the Court

WHEN ALICE heard her name called, she jumped up in such a hurry that she not only upset her nearest neighbors but toppled over all the jurymen.

"Poor little things!" she said, quite tenderly; and she picked them up, one by one, and set them back in the jury-box.

"The trial cannot go on," said the King, in a very solemn voice, "until all the jurymen are back in their proper places — *all*," he repeated, staring hard at Alice as he spoke.

Alice looked again at the jury-box and

saw that, in her haste, she had put poor little Bill the Lizard head downwards in his seat. The Lizard was waving his tail about in a helpless fashion being unable to move, and she very quickly lifted him up and put him right.

As soon as the jury had recovered, their slates and pencils were handed to them, and they began to write busily — all except the Lizard who sat with his mouth open, gazing up at the roof of the court.

"What do you know about this business?" the King said.

"Nothing," said Alice.

"Nothing whatever?" persisted the King.

"Nothing whatever," said Alice, glancing in the direction of the Knave of Hearts.

"That's very important," said the King, turning to the jury. "Write it down."

"His Majesty means 'unimportant'," the White Rabbit interrupted hastily, and he frowned and winked at the King. "Unimportant, you mean *unimportant,* your Majesty!"

Alice saw that some of the jurymen wrote "important" on their slates, while others wrote "unimportant".

"Not that it matters," she said to herself. "It's all nonsense anyway."

At this moment, the King called out "Silence!" and read out from a small black book: *Rule Forty-two: All persons more than a mile high to leave the court."*

Everybody looked at Alice.

"I'm not a mile high," said Alice.

"You are," said the King.

"Nearly two miles high," added the Queen.

"I shan't go," said Alice. "I think you invented that rule."

The King turned pale, and shut his black-book quickly. "Consider your verdict," he said to the jury, in a low trembling voice.

"They can't, your Majesty," the White Rabbit interrupted again. "There's more evidence to come. This paper has just been picked up!"

"What's in it?" asked the Queen.

"I haven't opened it yet," said the White

Rabbit, jumping up and waving the paper about. "But it seems to be a letter, written by the prisoner to — to somebody."

"Who is it addressed to?" asked one of the jurymen, "We must know that for evidence."

"Nobody," said the White Rabbit. "There's nothing written on the outside." He unfolded the paper as he spoke, and added, "It isn't a letter, after all, it's a set of verses."

"Are they in the prisoner's handwriting?" asked the King.

"No," replied the White Rabbit, looking both puzzled and disappointed.

"Then he must have imitated somebody else's hand," said the King. And all the jurymen looked pleased.

"That's not fair," Alice thought, but wisely she kept her thoughts to herself, and smiled instead at the Knave of Hearts.

"Please, your Majesty," said the Knave, "I didn't write it, and they can't prove it. There's no name signed at the end."

"If you didn't sign it," said the King, "that only makes it worse. It proves that you were up to some mischief — like stealing tarts."

Everybody clapped at this, and the King bowed slightly.

"That proves he is guilty," said the Queen.

"What nonsense!" cried Alice. "You haven't even read the verses."

"Read them," said the King.

The White Rabbit put on his spectacles, and began to read some of the verses on the paper at great speed.

The first one went something like this:
"They told me you had been to her,
And mentioned me to him:
She gave me a good character,
But said I could not swim."

Alice could scarcely stop herself interrupting as the Rabbit read on and on, each verse sillier than the one before. Yet when the Rabbit at last finished, the King said, "That's the most important piece of evidence we have heard yet."

"If anyone here can explain these ridiculous verses," said Alice boldly, "I'll — I'll give him a prize . . ."

By now she was so big that she didn't really mind what she said to the King.

"I seem to find meaning in them," said the King mildly, taking the paper from the White Rabbit, and studying it with great seriousness. "You can't swim, can you?" he added, addressing the Knave.

The Knave shook his head sadly. "Do I look as if I could swim?" he asked pathetically.

"Indeed he doesn't," thought Alice.

"How could he, being made of cardboard?"

"There is something here — in verse three," went on the King. *"I gave her one, they gave him two"* — that means the tarts, of course."

"It does not," said Alice.

"It does!" screamed the Queen, and she threw an inkstand at the Lizard as she spoke, for he had stopped making any attempt to write on his slate with one finger.

"Let the jury consider their verdict," the King said, for about the twentieth time that day.

"No, no!" interrupted the Queen furiously. "Sentence first — verdict afterwards."

"Stuff and nonsense!" said Alice loudly.

"Hold your tongue!" snapped the Queen, turning purple.

"I won't," said Alice.

"Off with her head!" the Queen shouted at the top of her voice. Nobody moved.

"Who cares for you?" cried Alice, who had by now grown to her full size. "Why, you're nothing but a pack of cards!"

At this the whole pack rose up into the air, and came flying down upon her.

Alice gave a little scream, half in fright and half in anger. She tried to beat them off — and found herself lying on the bank, with her head in her sister's lap.

Her sister brushed away the dead leaves that had fluttered down from the tree on to Alice's face.

"Wake up, Alice dear," she said. "You've been asleep for such a long time."

"I've had such a curious dream," Alice told her, sitting up. "Would you like to hear about it?"

Her sister nodded, and Alice began to tell her all she could remember of her strange adventures. "I know it began with the White Rabbit," she said, "and me running after it and falling down the rabbit-hole. Then there was the mouse and the Duchess and oh, so many other strange creatures."

On and on she talked, until at length her sister kissed her, and said, "It really was a very curious dream, dear. But now you must run in to your tea. It's getting ever so late."

So Alice got up and ran off, thinking while she ran, what a wonderful dream it had been.

But her sister sat still on the bank, her chin cupped in her hand, watching the setting sun, and thinking about little Alice and her adventures.

As she sat there, the whole place around her became alive with the strange creatures of her sister's dream.

The long grass rustled at her feet as the White Rabbit hurried by; and she could hear the frightened Mouse splashing in the pool and squeaking in protest as soon as it heard about Dinah.

So she continued to sit there, content to be in Alice's Wonderland for a few magic moments.

GORDON KING

Born in London in 1939, Gordon King spent
the war years in Scotland and achieved
considerable success as a child in major art
competitions. After training at Reading
University Art School he spent three years at
the Carlton Artists Studio before becoming a
freelance illustrator working for a wide range
of book and magazine publishers. In 1967 he
moved to Buckinghamshire and set up a
studio in the village of Chalfont St Peter. He
is married and has three children who
frequently model for him. Gordon King has
staged two one-man exhibitions. His paint-
ings hang in various major art galleries and
have been featured on television.